CATHERINE SEFTON

THE SKELETON CLUB

Illustrated by Maureen Bradley

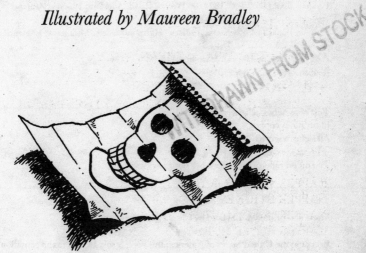

PUFFIN BOOKS

PUFFIN BOOKS

Published by the Penguin Group
Penguin Books Ltd, 27 Wrights Lane, London W8 5TZ, England
Penguin Books USA Inc., 375 Hudson Street, New York, New York 10014, USA
Penguin Books Australia Ltd, Ringwood, Victoria, Australia
Penguin Books Canada Ltd, 10 Alcorn Avenue, Toronto, Ontario, Canada M4V 3B2
Penguin Books (NZ) Ltd, 182–190 Wairau Road, Auckland 10, New Zealand

Penguin Books Ltd, Registered Offices: Harmondsworth, Middlesex, England

First published by Hamish Hamilton Ltd 1995
Published in Puffin Books 1997
10 9 8 7 6 5 4 3 2 1

Filmset in Baskerville

Made and printed in England by Clays Ltd, St Ives plc

1. How Pigface got his name

THIS IS WHAT happened when Pigface
came to our school and tangled with
Jerome's Skeleton Club. My name is
Conor Doran and I know what went
on because I was there.

It was Friday afternoon and we were
in class with Miss Brady, when a
woman arrived in a car. Miss Brady
went out of class to speak to her.

"Just keep quiet and read, you lot!"
Miss Brady said, and she went out into
the corridor, leaving the door ajar so
she could hear us if we started
creating.

"What is it this time, little Doran?"
Emma Bright asked, poking me with
the end of her ruler.

"Give over Emma," I said. "How
should I know?"

"'Cause you're a nosey little
Doran!" Emma said.

Then Nuala shouted out, "There's a
fat kid in that car."

Nuala has one of the seats near the
window, and she was standing up and
making faces at the fat kid.

Everyone crowded up to the window, trying to get a look at the fat kid. He had pushed himself down in the front seat of the car. He was pretending he didn't know we were all looking at him, but he was red in the face like a ripe tomato.

Emma banged the window at him, and then he had to look round.

He had a fat piggy face and a big snout. That is just what he looked like, a piggy.

"He looks like a piggy!" Jerome said, with a grin.

"Pigface!" Emma shouted, picking up on it quickly. She's like that. She is a little thin thing which is no surprise when you see her mother at their shop. Emma is always the first when it comes to mixing it, but this time even she didn't know what she was starting.

"Pigface! Pigface! Pigface!" Emma and Nuala and their lot were chanting.

"Children!" Miss Brady said.

She'd come back in, which wasn't surprising considering the row Emma's lot were making.

There was a real scuttle! Suddenly everybody was back in their seats, trying to look as if they hadn't been out of them.

"Is that one coming here, Miss?" Emma asked.

"He looks like a wee piggy!" Nuala said, with a giggle.

Nuala isn't too bright. She should have kept her mouth shut. She might have known talk like that would make Miss Brady mad.

Jerome caught the look on Miss Brady's face, and he whispered to Emma to tell Nuala to keep her mouth shut, but it was too late.

Miss Brady let us have it!

I don't remember what she said because I was too busy sitting up straight and trying to look as if I had nothing to do with it. I wouldn't have been up at the window if Emma and Nuala hadn't started it. I wouldn't have been shouting "Pigface" only everybody else was and it feels odd if you don't do what everybody else is doing.

"If that boy walks in this door, you'll be polite as polite to him and you'll be friends with him or you'll have me to answer to!" Miss Brady said grimly. "Mind that now!"

Then she walked across the room and stood just beside Jerome's desk.

"Mind that now!" she repeated, glaring at Jerome and Eamonn and me who were sitting behind him. She said it as though it was meant for everybody in the room, but everyone knew it wasn't. It was meant for the Skeleton Club.

I sat still, looking the other way so I wouldn't catch her eye. Eamonn was squirming a bit, but Jerome never blinked. He sat there very quiet,

6

playing with his pencil case, tapping it
almost soundlessly on the desk top,
right in front of her.

"Stop that, Jerome!" Miss Brady
snapped.

7

Jerome let the case fall on the desk, but he didn't look at Miss Brady. Jerome sat staring straight in front of him. He was dead cool!

It was one up to Jerome, proving that he was too smart to let her catch him doing anything.

Miss Brady was mean for the rest of the day and we all put it down to the Pigface business. So Pigface had made a bad start with the Skeleton Club, nearly getting Jerome into trouble.

We were on our way home down the Wrack Road, when my cousin Big Annie Toner started on at me.

"Your friend Jerome is a bully, Conor!" she said.

"Just the same, he keeps things right round here!" I said.

"Right for who?" Big Annie said. "You want to watch out for yourself,

Conor. Jerome will get you in big big trouble one day."

"Who says?" I said.

"I say," she said. "You think that what Jerome says goes, and you trail round after him like a wee lamb. If he told you to stand on your head in the bog you would do it! You should tell him you don't want to be in his Skeleton Club."

"Wise up, Annie!" I said. "I have to be in it. The ones who aren't in it get bashed."

"You all act scared of Jerome because he's big. But he's stupid, Jerome is! He gets caught out, like he did with the Taxes," Big Annie said.

The Taxes was when Jerome said the Skeleton Club would protect everybody for 10p each Tax, like the Government does. It was a really good

9

idea but some of them wouldn't give the 10p and somebody told Miss Brady. There was trouble and Jerome had to stop the Taxes, and Miss Brady made him give the 10ps back. Jerome said it was Donkey Newell who told on us so Jerome punched Donkey behind the bike sheds. Titchy Donkey Newell did what he always does. He kicks, which is why he is called Donkey. He tried kicking Jerome, but we all waded in and taught him a lesson for kicking. Kicking isn't fighting fair.

"Jerome isn't stupid," I said, uneasily.

"Well, you're brighter than he is anyway, Conor Doran. If you and the others got together and stood up for yourselves you'd be all right, but you're all too scared of Jerome to do it."

"Thanks for nothing!" I told her.

"That's girls' talk, that is! Girls never do anything. Boys have to do the fighting, and nobody is going to tackle Jerome. Why don't you take on Jerome if you're so fussed?"

"Maybe I will," she said, blinking at me through her double-glazed glasses. Then she splodged off down the Wrack Road in her sixteen-ton-load-bearing welly boots, which she needs because that is just about what she weighs.

She is big, but she is a girl. I reckoned she didn't mean to do anything about Jerome except talk. It would have been different if she was a boy and could do something, but girls never do.

Jerome already had her name down on his Skeleton Club List along with Donkey Newell. They were both going to be dealt with when we had the time, because the Honour of the Skeleton Club was at stake.

The whole point in having a Skeleton Club is that people do what we say, and if they don't they know the Skeleton Club will get them. Miss Brady banned the Skeleton Club after the Taxes, but we went on having it, so we could sort out people like Pigface when they came spoiling our school on us.

2. *Pigface gets the Skull Sign*

THE FOLLOWING MONDAY Pigface turned
up at school.

He had a Bugs Bunny bag. The bag
had his lunch in it. Nobody round
Ballygelget or Ballyculter ever had a
lunch bag like that, except in
Reception Class.

"We've a new Primary 7 today!"
Miss Brady told everyone cheerfully.
"This is Walter Rowen. Say 'Hello
Walter!'"

"Hello Walter!" everyone said.

No one was brave enough to say,
Hello Pigface instead, because

14

Miss Brady would have gone mad.

Pigface muttered something that might have been "hello".

"I know you'll all do your bit to make Walter feel welcome in Ballygelget," Miss Brady said brightly. "Now, we've got to find Walter a seat."

She sent Pigface to sit behind me, and just in front of Big Annie. I suppose she was hoping Annie would look after him. Annie sucks up to Miss Brady.

Jerome passed me a note in Emma's handwriting:

WHAT'S THE SMELL?

Jerome had written the answer:

PIG!

We passed it right round the room,

15

so everyone knew. Donkey Newell scrunched it up and threw it in the bin. I don't think Jerome saw him.

We went out to the yard at breaktime, and so did Pigface.

"Wait'll you see this, Doran!" Jerome said, nudging me, and he went up to Pigface, who was standing there looking stupid.

"Hi-ya, pal!" Jerome said. "I'm Jerome Hardy."

Pigface looked at him. They were measuring each other up. They were about the same size, which means both of them were bigger than anybody else in our school except Annie, and I reckon that is what had got Jerome going. Jerome is used to being bigger than anyone there ever was.

"Miss Brady says we've got to be nice to you," Jerome said. "So we're

going to let you play with us."

"I'm not!" Emma said.

"You *want* to play with us, don't you?" Jerome said, standing right close up to Pigface, so Pigface couldn't duck out of the talk.

17

Pigface didn't say anything. He looked worried. That wasn't surprising because Jerome has muscles through helping his daddy with the garage.

"You're *going* to play with us, like she said," Jerome told him, and he told me to get the ball and lay out the coats for our football.

"Doran is my side-kick," Jerome told Pigface. "That means he does what I say, and he has my protection. Okay? So you don't mess with Doran!"

"Make him the ball!" somebody shouted.

"Oh no," said Jerome. "We're going to be nice and play."

Pigface still didn't say anything. He must have known something was coming, but he didn't know what it was.

"You play football, don't you?"

Jerome asked Pigface.

Pigface nodded.

"That's good," said Jerome. "We have a good team and we beat the Anlee School and the Cubs and the B.B. from Scoilocktown. I'm Captain of our team, and I want to see how good you are, so I can consider you for selection." He grinned at me, and he winked.

We knew what to do. We'd done it before.

We stuck Pigface in the middle and no one passed to him and when he got the ball everybody tackled him, his own side and the other side.

Jerome got him three times, and Eamonn bashed him on the fence, and I did one of my Doran-busters on him.

The next time Jerome got the ball Pigface went mad.

Jerome was running with the ball and Pigface stuck his foot out. Over went Jerome, bang, nose down on the playground.

That was it!

We collared Pigface and held onto him; me and Eamonn and Gerry and Sam Elkins and Dopey and Goodman and Jamesy Scott all piled in on him. I was last man in so I was on top, sitting on his head, holding him down for Jerome.

"Get off him, Doran!" Jerome said, and he yanked me off, nearly breaking my arm.

Pigface got to his feet, and stood there with his fists clenched, glaring at Jerome.

"See you?" Jerome said, stepping up to him and grabbing Pigface by the shirt. "You're dead!"

"Okay," Pigface said, his eyes glittering. "If you want a fight, you'll get it!"

He took a poke at Jerome. It was a real windmiller of a punch and Jerome ducked back and it missed.

"Now you're for it, Pigface!" I shouted, waiting for Jerome to clout him, but Jerome didn't.

"You needn't think I'm hitting you," Jerome said, standing back with a grin on his face. "You've *them* on your side. The teachers and all. I'm not hitting you. I wouldn't dirty my hands. But you've had it!" and he repeated, "You're dead, Pigface!" several times, so everyone would hear.

"I think you're rotten, Jerome!" Big Annie said. She'd come up with Donkey Newell from our form and Sharon and Lottie from Primary 6, and the McAuleys, who are the ones she pals around with at school. Her lot are yellow, and they are all on the Skeleton Club List.

"Then *you* and your wee friends play with him!" Jerome said.

Annie ignored him. She tried talking to Pigface and calling him Walter, but he wasn't having any, and told her to get knotted.

Pigface went off to have a sulk somewhere, and he stayed there until he discovered that somebody had nicked his Bugs Bunny bag with his lunch in. It was in the dustbin where Emma had put it but we didn't show it to him until just before going in time.

Jerome came up to me.

"Doran!" he said. "You get busy. This is a job for the Skeleton Club! Pigface thinks he is big and he can

23

throw his weight around in school because he has Miss Brady on his side. We've got to show him it isn't going to be like that. We're not having any big new kid take over this school from us. There's only room for one leader here, and it is me!"

I did our Skull Sign for Jerome on a bit of my jotter. He folded it sixways like we do. Jerome put the Skull on Pigface's desk, and made sure everyone saw him doing it, so they would know it was Skeleton Club Official.

Pigface saw it when he sat down. He didn't know what it meant, though I think he guessed.

The rules of the Skeleton Club were that the people Jerome picked on had to be given the Sign. If they didn't know what it was, they soon found out. It was like the Black Spot in *Treasure*

Island that Miss Brady read us, only better, because Jerome's Black Spot was a Skull with a grin. If anybody sneaked we could just say it is a picture and so what?

Pigface got our Skull Sign, and that meant everyone knew Pigface was doomed.

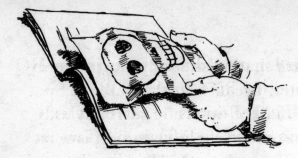

3. The Skeleton Club

JEROME WAS WORLD Commander of the Skeleton Club and Gerry Brennan was Major General and Eamonn Brennan was Operations Officer and the others were Sticky and me. We got doing the messages for the other three. We were only let in because Jerome said there had to be five. Jerome said it meant we were like the five fingers on a Skeleton's hand, closing round the throats of all enemies. There were only four of us when it came to the Pigface business because Sticky had mumps.

Jerome called a Skeleton Club

Meeting after dinner time, in our HQ round the Bike Shed.

"Pigface thinks he can fight us!" Jerome told the Meeting. "If we let him away with that they'll all be doing it, and that will be the end of the Skeleton Club."

"Well, we ought to do him," Eamonn Brennan said. "Give him a mud sandwich like we gave Donkey Newell."

"Only what about Miss Brady?" I said.

If Miss Brady heard Pigface got done like Donkey, she would know it was the Skeleton Club still going on, after being banned. She had told us there would be real trouble if she caught us at it again after the Taxes.

"He'll be too scared to tell Miss Brady," Gerry said.

"Only supposing he isn't?" I said.

"You're yellow," Gerry said. "Who's scared of Miss Brady anyway? What can she do? If Pigface won't talk, she can't prove it was us."

"And we'll fix it so Pigface won't talk," Jerome said, grimly. "We'll get him after school."

We didn't know what way Pigface would be going home after school, but Jerome said Pigface was a stranger and he'd be sticking to the roads. Jerome said we could use the fields and cut him off just where we wanted to.

"You be our spies," Jerome told Nuala and Emma. "You slow him up coming out of school, so we can get in front. Then we see what way he is going and we set our ambush and he will walk right in to it."

Nuala and Emma must have

blabbed, because Big Annie found out.

"Don't you dare ambush him!" she told Jerome in the lane.

"What'll you do, Droopy Drawers?" Jerome asked. "Tell Miss Brady like the last time?"

Jerome thought it was Big Annie who egged Donkey on to tell on the Taxes, though he couldn't prove it. Donkey and Big Annie probably told Miss Brady we were taking all the little one's dinner money which is how we got banned. All we were doing was making sure the little ones didn't get bashed by bigger ones without our permission, and they paid us Taxes so we would bash the bigger ones for them, so the Taxes were fair pay. Our Skeleton Club was like a Police Force for our school, seeing no one stepped out of line.

"Pigface might give you more than you bargain for," Big Annie said.

"He'll get what is coming to him," Jerome told her.

So we had our ambush.

The four of us got Pigface round the

back of Coulter's Bend and we had the
old Bugs Bunny bag off him and we
rolled him in the muck and showed
him Jerome was boss.

Pigface was crying, just like Donkey Newell was when we did it to him.

"You go home, now, Cry-Baby!" Jerome told him. "And you open your mouth one time about this and you'll find you have no teeth in it the next day."

So that saw Pigface off.

Jerome thought he would be too scared to come to school the next day, and maybe we were rid of him for good.

I was coming down the Wrack Road to our house when Big Annie got me. She must have been waiting in the hedge.

"I heard what Jerome did, Conor," she told me. "Everybody's had enough of Jerome picking on people."

"Who is everybody?" I said. "You and Donkey and the wee ones?"

Donkey and Big Annie didn't like fighting, and the wee ones like the McAuleys were too small to tackle the Skeleton Club, so I didn't think Jerome had much to worry about.

"If Jerome does it again, he'll get what's coming to him," Big Annie said, and she went off. Then she came back and she said, "You can tell Jerome that from me, too!"

When I told Jerome he said, "So she's challenging us to do Pigface again?"

"Yeh," I said.

"So we will!" he said.

We thought we had to do it, because nobody had ever said things like that to the Skeleton Club before.

4. The Pigface Patrol

PIGFACE TURNED UP at school the next day in clean clothes, so somebody had washed the muck off. We reckoned he'd been too scared to tell his mother how the muck got on, so that was all right.

He came in the class late and sat down without even looking at us.

"What a pong!" Nuala said.

"It's him," Emma said.

"I'm not sitting near him," Nuala said.

Pigface went red again, but he didn't say a word. Then Miss Brady came

34

in and that stopped it.

Breaktime he didn't join in the football.

He was down the bike sheds on his own and then the little McAuleys and Donkey Newell were talking to him. We didn't pay them any heed.

Lunchtime, Eamonn went up to Pigface in the playground.

"Jerome says we'll be seeing you again this afternoon, Pigface," Eamonn said. "We just thought we'd tell you so you'd know. And don't try going a different way, because we'll get you just the same."

Pigface slouched off round the back where Big Annie and Donkey were with the little ones. They were playing some silly game making lists of people. That is what Eamonn said it was anyway, when he was spy-reporting to

35

Jerome. Eamonn said Pigface was all
red round the eyes as though he had
been crying.

Big Annie came hunting for Jerome
later, when she'd finished wiping
Pigface's cheeks and blowing his Piggy
snout for him with her hanky.

"You leave Walter alone, Jerome!"
she said. "You're dead mean!" She
was all worked up about it.

"Keep out of this, Annie! Cry-Baby
Pigface has been asking for it, and now
he knows he's going to get it!" Jerome
said.

"I'm warning you . . ." Big Annie
began.

"Oh no!" Jerome broke in, dead
cool. "I'm the one that's warning you
and your mate Donkey. No telling
Miss Brady on us this time, or else!"

"I've had enough of you, Jerome
Hardy!" Big Annie told him. "First it
was Donkey you picked on and now
you're picking on Walter and I am sick
of it, because you're spoiling this
school for everybody!"

She was blazing mad.

Jerome just laughed at her.

"What'll you do?" he sneered. "You and titchy little tell-tale Donkey Newell? Go running to Miss Brady again?"

"Oh no," she said.

"Scaredy-cats!" Jerome said. "Cry-babies!"

"You *like* making people cry, don't you Jerome?" Big Annie said.

"You go to Miss Brady about it and you'll be crying too!" Jerome warned her.

"Well, we'll just see about that, Jerome!" Big Annie said. "We'll just see what happens if you lay another finger on Walter!"

"She's too scared to go to Miss Brady, because she knows what she'd get from us after!" Jerome told us. "But we're not letting her off with it. We're going to do Pigface just like we said we would, then everybody will know that the Skeleton Club still means business, and prove we're not afraid of Miss Brady or anybody!"

So that made certain sure we weren't going to let up on Pigface.

The Skeleton Club Plan to Get Pigface for Good was definitely on.

After school we headed off for Coulter's Bend, which is just round the corner after the lane forks, by the cow field.

Jerome had it all planned out. Eamonn had a shovel in the hedge and he was going to shovel some cow dung on. We were going to wait behind the hedge. When Pigface came along he would think the Skeleton Club wasn't there and then we'd jump out and splosh him with it and he would be cow dung all over this time.

"It's going to be really good," Eamonn said.

What none of us expected was Big Annie's Pigface Patrol!

Pigface came down the lane all right, but with him he had Big Annie, two McAuleys, and Liam and Donkey. Liam is a Primary 3 and he doesn't count.

They came down the lane toward us, in a group.

"Hey! Jerome!" Big Annie called.

She must have guessed we were hiding there.

Jerome came out from behind the hedge.

"This lane's barred," he said.

"Oh yeh?" Annie said. "Who says?"

"The Skeleton Club," Jerome said. "The lane's barred to everybody but Pigface."

Then he said to Pigface, "You're all right, Pigface. It's on the way to your house, so you can pass, only nobody else. So we're sticking up for you, aren't we? Sticking up for your rights, so you can get safe home to your mammy!"

Pigface said nothing.

"We're all going to his house," Big Annie announced.

Jerome just laughed at her. "Who are we?" he said. "You and Donkey?"

"No," Big Annie said. "Me and all these ones!"

She shouted something, and round the corner came about half the Primary 4's and most of the Primary 5's and a whole crowd of the tiny ones that she must have rounded up. That is what her lists had been about.

"You touch Walter and you touch the lot of us," she told Jerome.

"You think your wee Pigface Patrol can fight us?" Jerome said. "Catch yourself on, Annie."

"Nobody's fighting anybody," Annie said. "We're just walking Walter back to his house."

And Donkey said, "Come on," and started toward us.

"You'll get it!" Jerome shouted.

"I'm warning you, Donkey. You want another mud sandwich and you'll get it. There's enough for all of you."

Eamonn came out from behind the hedge with the shovel of cow dung. Gerry was with Eamonn, and I was just behind Jerome.

"I'm telling you this lane is barred!" Jerome repeated. "It is Skeleton Club Official! I'm warning you."

I was doing a count. There were fourteen of them, not counting the Reception ones, and there were only four of us. That's the first time I thought it might be going wrong for Jerome.

Big Annie and Pigface and Donkey had linked arms and they came right up to Jerome and Gerry Brennan, bringing the whole pack of little ones with them.

"If you touch one of us, you touch everybody, Jerome!" Big Annie said. "So you'd better just let us pass, hadn't you?"

Eamonn Brennan had stepped back. He climbed up onto the bank of the ditch, with his shovel of cow dung. He was going to bomb them with the cow dung, and then we'd give them their mud sandwiches later.

"Move, Jerome," Big Annie said.

Jerome reached out and grabbed the strap of Annie's schoolbag as she went to go past him. He looked as if he was going to hit her.

"Let me go, Jerome," Annie said.

"Let her go, Jerome," Pigface said.

There was a long silence. Jerome was sizing them up, and the bad thing was Pigface was as big as he was. Annie was bigger than Gerry Brennan, and then there were the McAuleys and Donkey, and all the little ones as well.

"Okay," Jerome said. "I'll let you go. But remember. The lane is still barred by Skeleton Club order. I'm letting you go, but that doesn't mean it is unbarred."

And he stood aside.

They all went past him, down the lane.

"Fire!" Jerome yelled to Eamonn.

Eamonn aimed the cow dung on the shovel at Big Annie and Pigface.

That's what he *meant* to do anyway, but it went wrong.

Donkey was by the ditch and he made a half grab at the shovel as Eamonn swung it back. The result was the cow dung flew off the shovel and all over Jerome's face and down his clothes and everywhere.

Jerome went raving mad. The next thing we knew he was after Pigface, kicking and punching and yelling, and when Jerome goes like that odd things happen.

And an odd thing happened.

Jerome went for Pigface, and *everybody* went for Jerome.

All the little tiny Primary 4s and Primary 5s piled in together and Jerome went down with the whole lot of them clinging onto him. Only Big Annie and Pigface stayed out of it, and

they were the big ones. It was the small ones who tackled Jerome. I couldn't understand that.

"Rescue!" Gerry Brennan shouted and he charged, but he didn't charge far. Big Annie is much much bigger than Gerry, and she had Pigface beside her.

"Clear off, Gerry," she said. "And take your brother with you." So Gerry and Eamonn cleared off.

Then she told the Pigface Patrol to get up off Jerome. He got up crying and panting with anger at being done over by a pack of babies.

"Go home, Jerome, or I'll set them on you again!" Big Annie warned him.

Jerome had had enough. He belted off.

"You go home too, Conor Doran!" she told me.

Annie and Pigface and Donkey and the others thought they had won, but I wasn't so sure. On my way home I was thinking that it would be different next day.

Annie could get half the school ganged up and stop Jerome one day, but she couldn't do it *every* day, and Jerome would go on being Jerome. He would still be bigger than anybody and still be Boss and he'd make us do what he wanted because that is what the Skeleton Club was all about.

So I was worried about what would happen next day, and I would have been even more worried if I was Big Annie, or Pigface, because they were the ones he'd be out to get.

If I was them I'd have stayed off school!

5. Jerome

"WHERE'S JEROME?" Gerry said. "Is he coming, or is he chicken?"

It was next morning before school and we were in the bicycle shed, but Jerome wasn't there.

"I bet he's planning something," I said.

Then Big Annie and Donkey Newell came up.

"Have you seen your friend Jerome?" Big Annie said. "Because Nuala's going round saying he is a cry-baby and he told his mammy on us!"

49

The bell went and we had to go in and Miss Brady started us on our Earth Project. Then the door burst open. It was Jerome's mammy, Mrs Hardy, and she was dragging Jerome behind her.

"Come in here, Jerome!" she said, and she marched Jerome up to the desk, and plonked him in front of Miss Brady.

"Late again, Jerome?" said Miss Brady.

"He's nearly not here at all!" Jerome's mammy said. She was red in the face and fuming. It was really interesting to look at her. She has big pink specs and I thought they were going to bounce off her nose when her jaw got going.

"Can I help you, Mrs Hardy?" said Miss Brady.

50

"This wee boy," said Jerome's mammy, "this poor wee boy was set upon by a whole crowd of your children and covered in cow muck and sent home to me yesterday crying his heart out. And what I want to know is what are you going to do about it, Miss Brady?"

Miss Brady didn't speak for a minute. She took a deep breath, and seemed to think, and then she seemed to think again, and what she said wasn't what we expected at all.

"We can't have a poor little boy like Jerome being bullied by other rough children, can we?" Miss Brady said, looking Jerome hard in the face, so he'd know right off what she *wasn't* saying to his mammy, that she might have . . . "Now tell me, Jerome, which children did it?"

Jerome went beetroot. He knew if he talked he would have to tell Miss Brady that kids like Donkey and the two McAuleys and the Primary 4s and Primary 5s had done for him. Miss Brady would tell his mammy what babies they were, compared to Jerome.

"You tell her!" Jerome's mammy ordered him, but Jerome just blushed red. He knew we were all laughing at him, even Nuala and Emma, and there was nothing he *could* say that wouldn't make it worse.

"The wee boy is scared stiff of your big bullies!" Mrs Hardy told Miss Brady, and she didn't seem to notice that her Jerome was bigger than almost everybody in the room.

"Oh dear," said Miss Brady. "I'm afraid we have some terribly rough elements in the class. Poor dear little Jerome."

It went on like that.

I don't know how Miss Brady kept her face straight, but she did. The end up was that Miss Brady told Mrs Hardy that she would keep a special eye on Jerome to see that none of the big bullies got him and Jerome's mammy went off.

Then we got on with our lesson.

At break Miss Brady asked, "Would you like to stay safe in here with me, Jerome, just for today?"

Jerome said he wouldn't.

"Well, you're all to be nice to Jerome, or you'll have me to answer to!" Miss Brady said, and she went off grinning like a cat, because she knew fine well the way it was.

We went out to the playground.

Nuala came up to him.

"You let a pack of babies lick you, Jerome," she said. "You're no use."

"Yeh," said Emma Bright. "Girls and big babies, and then you brought your mammy into school to complain."

"My mammy wouldn't *not* come," Jerome mumbled, angrily. He was almost crying. "I didn't want her coming. I told her not to."

"Don't worry your wee head, Jerome," Big Annie said. "I won't let any of the little babies in Primary 3 bully you."

54

"I'll punch your face in for you, Annie!" Jerome broke out, his eyes glistening with tears.

"You'll need to punch me too, Jerome," Pigface said.

"Me too," said Donkey. "And the McAuleys. And everybody else. No one's on your side any more, because they all know what you're made of."

And Jerome didn't punch Pigface.

"Cry-Baby!" Nuala said to Jerome.

"You're yellow, Jerome," said Gerry Brennan and Emma to Jerome.

"You're out of the Skeleton Club, Brennan!" Jerome shouted.

"What Skeleton Club? That's kid's stuff!" Gerry told him.

"You're on my list, Brennan!" Jerome yelled at him and Miss Brady heard him and she came out and asked Jerome if he was all right.

"I wouldn't want your mammy coming in to scold me again, Jerome," she told him. "Just you come to me if anybody is nasty and I'll look after you, dear." Then she fished out her hanky and dried his eyes for him, and told him to blow his nose.

That about finished Jerome with everybody.

Big Annie says there's not going to be Skeleton Clubs or Gangs that bully people at our school any more and if anyone tries to start one *everyone* will come together and stop it. Big Annie says people shouldn't bully people, and I think Big Annie is right!

She's not bad for a girl, even if she is my cousin.

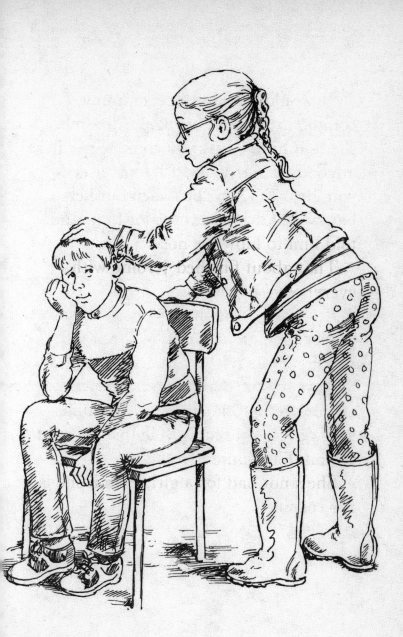

READ MORE IN PUFFIN

For children of all ages, Puffin represents quality and variety – the very best in publishing today around the world.

For complete information about books available from Puffin – and Penguin – and how to order them, contact us at the appropriate address below. Please note that for copyright reasons the selection of books varies from country to country.

On the worldwide web: www.penguin.co.uk

In the United Kingdom: Please write to *Dept. EP, Penguin Books Ltd, Bath Road, Harmondsworth, West Drayton, Middlesex UB7 ODA*

In the United States: Please write to *Consumer Sales, Penguin USA, P.O. Box 999, Dept. 17109, Bergenfield, New Jersey 07621-0120*. VISA and MasterCard holders call 1-800-253-6476 to order Penguin titles

In Canada: Please write to *Penguin Books Canada Ltd, 10 Alcorn Avenue, Suite 300, Toronto, Ontario M4V 3B2*

In Australia: Please write to *Penguin Books Australia Ltd, P.O. Box 257, Ringwood, Victoria 3134*

In New Zealand: Please write to *Penguin Books (NZ) Ltd, Private Bag 102902, North Shore Mail Centre, Auckland 10*

In India: Please write to *Penguin Books India Pvt Ltd, 706 Eros Apartments, 56 Nehru Place, New Delhi 110 019*

In the Netherlands: Please write to *Penguin Books Netherlands bv, Postbus 3507, NL-1001 AH Amsterdam*

In Germany: Please write to *Penguin Books Deutschland GmbH, Metzlerstrasse 26, 60594 Frankfurt am Main*

In Spain: Please write to *Penguin Books S. A., Bravo Murillo 19, 1° B, 28015 Madrid*

In Italy: Please write to *Penguin Italia s.r.l., Via Felice Casati 20, I–20124 Milano*

In France: Please write to *Penguin France S. A., 17 rue Lejeune, F–31000 Toulouse*

In Japan: Please write to *Penguin Books Japan, Ishikiribashi Building, 2–5–4, Suido, Bunkyo-ku, Tokyo 112*

In South Africa: Please write to *Longman Penguin Southern Africa (Pty) Ltd, Private Bag X08, Bertsham 2013*